A thief is on the

"Cal, give the babies their
to have to have a tim
exclaimed.

The chaos and confusion went on for a while,
until finally, Mrs. Gregory put on the *Happy
Baby Songs* CD, and the twins calmed down
and started twirling in place. Cal dropped
the silver rattle and started dancing too. Mrs.
Jacobs picked up the rattle and put it back on
the bookshelf, next to a row of encyclopedias.

Nancy and her friends played with the twins
for a little while longer. Just before five, the
girls started picking up the twins' toys.

Nancy frowned as she returned Squeak
Squeak to the book shelf. "Where's the silver
rattle?" she asked George. "I thought I saw
Mrs. Gregory put it here somewhere. Did you
move it?"

George smiled at Anna Lin, then turned to
Nancy and shook her head. "I didn't move it."

"I didn't move it either," Bess piped up.

Join the CLUE CREW
& solve these other cases!

NANCY DREW
AND THE CLUE CREW®

#23

Babysitting Bandit

BY CAROLYN KEENE

ILLUSTRATED BY MACKY PAMINTUAN

Aladdin

New York London Toronto Sydney

This book is a work of fiction. Any references to historical events, real people, or real locales are used fictitiously. Other names, characters, places, and incidents are the product of the author's imagination, and any resemblance to actual events or locales or persons, living or dead, is entirely coincidental.

⟡ ALADDIN

An imprint of Simon & Schuster Children's Publishing Division

1230 Avenue of the Americas, New York, NY 10020

First Aladdin paperback edition November 2009

Text copyright © 2009 by Simon & Schuster, Inc.

Illustrations copyright © 2009 by Macky Pamintuan

All rights reserved, including the right of reproduction in whole or in part in any form.

ALADDIN is a trademark of Simon & Schuster, Inc., and related logo is a registered trademark of Simon & Schuster, Inc.

NANCY DREW and related logos are registered trademarks of Simon & Schuster, Inc.

NANCY DREW AND THE CLUE CREW is a registered trademark of Simon & Schuster, Inc.

For information about special discounts for bulk purchases, please contact Simon & Schuster Special Sales at 1-866-506-1949 or business@simonandschuster.com.

The Simon & Schuster Speakers Bureau can bring authors to your live event. For more information or to book an event contact the Simon & Schuster Speakers Bureau at 1-866-248-3049 or visit our website at www.simonspeakers.com.

Designed by Lisa Vega

The text of this book was set in ITC Stone Informal.

Manufactured in the United States of America

10 9 8 7

Library of Congress Control Number 2008943892

ISBN 978-1-4169-7813-8

ISBN 978-1-4169-9702-3 (eBook)

1018 OFF

CONTENTS

CHAPTER ONE

Double Trouble

"What's in your backpack, Bess?" Nancy Drew asked as she skipped down the sidewalk.

"Yeah, it looks super full," George Fayne said, skipping along next to Nancy.

"It's my babysitting kit," Bess Marvin explained. She paused to hoist the bulging backpack higher on her shoulders, then started skipping again. "I have everything I need to take care of the twins: some of my old baby toys that I found in the attic. And books. And paper and crayons. And Togo."

"Togo?" George repeated.

"Togo is my stuffed tiger. When I was a baby, my parents would pretend it could talk to me, and I would do whatever it said. Like . . . 'Bess, eat your broccoli,' and, 'Bess, don't throw your sippy cup.'" She added, "I thought we could use it with the twins so they'll listen to us."

"Or maybe the twins are smart and they'll know stuffed tigers can't talk," George teased Bess.

George and Bess were cousins, although they had really different personalities. They looked different, too; George had short, curly brown hair and brown eyes, and Bess had long, blond hair and blue eyes.

Nancy and her friends were on their way to the Jacobses' house, which was just down the street from the Drews' house. Mrs. Jacobs had hired the three girls to be "mother's helpers" for her eighteen-month-old twins, Lily Mei and Anna Lin, whom she and her husband had adopted from China. A mother's helper was like a babysitter, except that the parent or parents stayed home while the mother's helper played with the baby—or, in this case, babies.

Mrs. Jacobs had asked Nancy, George, and Bess to watch Lily Mei and Anna Lin on Mondays, Wednesdays, and Fridays after school for a couple of hours so she could make phone calls and do chores. Mr. Jacobs worked in an office in downtown River Heights, so he usually didn't get home until dinnertime. The job would last for a few weeks, until Mrs. Jacobs's twelve-year-old daughter Margaret, was finished with a big science project. After that, Margaret would be able to take over with the twins.

They soon reached the Jacobses' house. They went up to the front door and rang the bell. A moment later, Mrs. Jacobs answered. Her long honey-colored hair tumbled loosely from a clip, and her jeans and black sweatshirt were splattered with what looked like mashed banana. A cell phone was pressed between her right ear and her shoulder.

"Oh hi, girls. You're right on time!" Mrs. Jacobs said.

Nancy peered through the door at the Jacobses'

living room. The twins were sitting on the floor, going through a black leather purse. One twin pulled out a slim gray wallet and dumped out all the money, credit cards, and receipts. The other twin tossed a tube of lipstick across the room. A silver pen followed, then a checkbook, then a pack of gum.

"I'll have to call you back," Mrs. Jacobs said into the phone. "Come in, come in," she said to the girls.

Nancy, George, and Bess entered the front hall, then followed Mrs. Jacobs as she stepped over a low baby gate into the living room.

"Lily Mei! Anna Lin! Look who's here!" Mrs. Jacobs called out brightly.

The twins stopped what they were doing and glanced up with curious expressions. They were identical, with the same large, brown eyes, small, pert noses, and shiny, chin-length black hair with bangs cut straight across their foreheads. They wore identical T-shirts and denim overalls embroidered with flowers, except that one twin had a purple tee and the other twin wore pink.

"Nancy, George, and Bess are going to be playing with you today," Mrs. Jacobs said to the twins. "Why don't you have a tea party while I talk to them, okay?"

She bent down quickly and scooped up the contents of her purse. Just as quickly, she got a toy tea set from a bookshelf and set it on the floor between the twins.

The twins got busy with the tea set. Mrs. Jacobs kept her eyes on them as she addressed the girls. "So you can see that they're kind of a handful," she said apologetically. "Anyway . . . let me go over everything with you. Just stop me if you have any questions."

"Okay," Nancy said. George and Bess nodded.

"The twins love to be read to. There's a bunch of books in a basket in the corner, there, and also up in their room," Mrs. Jacobs began. "Just watch that they don't rip the pages or draw on them. They like to finger paint, but they try to eat the paints, so we use vanilla pudding with food coloring mixed in it. I keep that in the fridge. Just make sure they're wearing their painting smocks, which are in their closet. As for toys . . . well, there are toys all over the house. But they do have their favorites.

"Like what?" George asked her.

Mrs. Jacobs got a few more toys from the bookshelf. One of them was a silver, moon-shaped rattle. The other was a little stuffed mouse toy. "The rattle belonged to Margaret when she was a baby," she said, smiling softly. "It's engraved with her name and birthday. The twins are really too old for rattles, but for some reason, they just love this one. As for the mouse . . . his name is Squeak Squeak.

6

They fight over him, so you have to tell them to share nicely. If they won't share, take him away. Oh, and if they're being kind of hyper and crazy, there's a CD on top of the CD player that calms them right down. It's called *Happy Baby Songs*."

"I brought some toys and stuff too," Bess said, setting her backpack on the ground.

"Oh, wonderful! The twins like to—oh, dear! Sir Barkalot! No, Sir Barkalot!" Mrs. Jacobs cried out.

A big, shaggy white dog leaped over the baby gate and tore through the living room. He opened his mouth and hungrily scooped up a plastic cookie from the twins' tea party. The babies began wailing.

"Bad dog!" Mrs. Jacobs chided Sir Barkalot. She reached into his mouth and pulled out the cookie, which was now covered with doggie-drool. "Oh, dear! You have to watch out for him," she told Nancy, George, and Bess. "*Everything* goes into his mouth. He'll try to eat toys, balls, shoes—even CDs."

"CDs?" Bess gasped.

"CDs. Lily Mei, Anna Lin, it's okay. Mommy got your cookie back from the doggie," Mrs. Jacobs reassured the twins. They snuffled and stopped crying.

Mrs. Jacobs continued giving Nancy, George, and Bess instructions about the twins. She told them about snacks, diaper changes—which she would handle—discipline, and safety. She showed them how to hook and unhook the baby gates.

"It's important that you never let the twins out of your sight," she finished. "They can get into trouble in about two seconds flat."

"Just like Sir Barkalot," Nancy noted.

"Exactly! Oh, and we have a kitty-cat, too. Pumpkin Pie."

"Meow!" the twins said at the same time.

Mrs. Jacobs beamed. "That's right—meow!

Anyway, she's around here somewhere."

"Mom, are there any banana muffins left, or did the little monsters eat them all?"

Nancy turned around. A girl with short, honey-colored hair came into the living room, followed by a blond girl and a redheaded boy.

"Margaret!" Mrs. Jacobs snapped. "Please do not refer to your sisters as 'little monsters.' We talked about that."

"Whatever. Are there any muffins left? Lacie and Matt and me are *starving*!" Margaret said.

"Lacie and Matt and *I*. Yes, we still have muffins. And there's some lemonade in the fridge." Mrs. Jacobs turned to the three girls. "Nancy, George, Bess . . . this is my daughter Margaret. These are her friends Lacie and Matt. They're doing a science project together."

The six kids exchanged hellos. Lily Mei and Anna Lin ran up to Margaret and threw their arms around her legs. "Mah-Mah!" they exclaimed happily.

Margaret patted their heads. "Yeah, hi," she

said, sounding bored. She glanced at Lacie and Matt and rolled her eyes.

"What? They're so *cute*," Lacie said.

"Yeah, they're way cuter than *my* sisters," Matt piped up.

"So you're stuck with the little monsters, huh?" Margaret said to Nancy, George, and Bess. "Good luck with that!"

Mrs. Jacobs put her hands on her hips. *"Margaret!"*

"Sorry, Mom. 'Kay, we're outta here. Muffins, people!" Margaret called out to her friends. They headed for the kitchen, which was separated from the living room by another baby gate.

"I'm sorry about that," Mrs. Jacobs said, lowering her voice to a whisper. "Margaret is having some . . . adjustment problems with Lily Mei and Ann Lin. She was an only child for twelve years, and it hasn't been easy for her." She gazed down at the silver, moon-shaped rattle, which one of the twins was now holding. "She's even mad that the twins play with her rattle."

George nodded. "I have two brothers, Sebastian and Scott. It's hard to share with them sometimes."

"Yeah, my sister Maggie can be a pain too," Bess agreed.

Mrs. Jacobs smiled. "So you understand. Anyway . . . oh my, where has the time gone?" she exclaimed, glancing at her watch. "Do you have any questions? No? Then why don't I leave you to play with the twins while I start dinner?"

"Sure," Nancy said. "We can have a tea party with them."

"Wonderful! I'll be right in there if you need me," Mrs. Jacobs said, pointing to the kitchen.

After she left, Nancy, George, and Bess sat down on the floor next to the twins. "Hi!" Bess said. "I'm Bess! And this is Nancy, and this is George."

The twins blinked at her. One of them wandered over to a pile of wooden blocks and began stacking them. The other one stood behind Nancy and peered over her shoulder.

"I'll pour some tea," Nancy said, picking up

the teapot and tipping it over one of the cups. "What do you want in your tea, Anna Lin? Sugar? Honey? Lemon? Milk? What about you, Lily Mei?" She put a pretend-lump of sugar in one of the cups.

"Which one's Lily Mei and which one's Anna Lin?" George whispered to Nancy. "They look exactly alike!"

Nancy frowned. "I'm pretty sure the one in purple is Lily Mei."

"No, I think the one in *pink* is Lily Mei," Bess whispered.

"Your tea is ready!" Nancy called out to Lily Mei, or whichever twin was playing with blocks.

Except . . . she wasn't there. She wasn't anywhere in the living room.

Nancy felt a rush of panic. Oh, no! She, George, and Bess had taken their eyes off Lily Mei for two seconds—and she had disappeared!

chaPTER TWo

Missing?

"Where's Lily Mei?" Nancy cried out, jumping to her feet.

George and Bess glanced around the living room. "She's gone!" Bess gasped.

"She couldn't have gone very far," George said worriedly.

Nancy realized that George was right. There were only two ways in or out of the living room—the kitchen in one direction and the hallway in the other—and they were both closed off by baby gates.

Nancy could see Mrs. Jacobs in the kitchen, washing dishes. Margaret and her friends were standing at the counter, pouring lemonade from a pitcher. None of them seemed to know what was happening with Lily Mei.

Was Lily Mei hiding somewhere in the living room? Nancy wondered.

Anna Lin was sitting quietly on the floor, nibbling on a pretend-cookie. She didn't seem to notice that her twin sister was missing.

"Bess, you watch Anna Lin. George and I are going to look for Lily Mei," Nancy said, trying to stay calm.

"Look where?" Bess asked her.

"She could be hiding behind the couch, or—"

Just then, the door bell rang. Nancy watched as Mrs. Jacobs turned off the kitchen faucet and stepped over the baby gate, into the living room. Sir Barkalot was right behind her, barking.

"I think that's my friend, Mrs.—*where's Lily Mei?*" Mrs. Jacobs demanded, stopping in her tracks.

Nancy gulped. So did George and Bess.

"She's . . . that is . . . ," Nancy began. She

didn't know how to tell Mrs. Jacobs that they had lost Lily Mei.

"Peek-a-boo!"

Lily Mei jumped out from behind the love seat. She burst into a fit of giggles. Anna Lin started giggling too. *So that's where Lily Mei was,* Nancy thought. *Whew!*

Mrs. Jacobs's expression relaxed. "Peek-a-boo to you, too, sweetheart!"

Anna Lin hid her face in her hands, then peered through her fingers. "Peep-a-goo!" she squealed.

"That's *peek-a-boo,* bunny. I forgot to mention that this is one of their favorite games," Mrs.

Jacobs said to Nancy, George, and Bess. The doorbell rang again. Sir Barkalot barked. "Oh, right! Excuse me, I've got to get that."

Mrs. Jacobs stepped over the baby gate into the hallway and opened the front door. Nancy saw a woman standing there along with a little boy. The boy was dressed in a green polo shirt, jeans—and a red cape.

Before Mrs. Jacobs had a chance to say hello, the boy rushed into the house and jumped over the baby gate, his cape flapping wildly behind him. Sir Barkalot bounded after him, barking.

"Look out, it's Super Sonic Man!" the boy yelled. The twins clapped and shrieked in delight.

"Cal! You come back here right this second!" the woman called out.

"Please don't worry about it, Sarah," Mrs. Jacobs said.

Mrs. Jacobs introduced her guests to the girls as her next-door neighbor Mrs. Gregory, and her five-year-old son, Cal. "He has a lot of energy," Mrs. Gregory apologized.

"Hey, you bad thieves! Give back the stolen treasure!" Cal demanded. He swooped down and grabbed the silver, moon-shaped rattle, which was lying on the floor next to the tea set. He held it up in the air and started running in circles around the living room. Sir Barkalot followed, barking.

First Lily Mei, then Anna Lin began crying and grabbing for the rattle. "Cal, give that back to the babies right this second!" Mrs. Gregory scolded him. But Cal continued running in circles, along with Sir Barkalot.

"It's okay, it's okay," Mrs. Jacobs said, kneeling down next to the twins. "Here, why don't you invite Squeak Squeak to come to your tea party?"

Wanting to be helpful, Nancy hurried over to the bookshelf and got Squeak Squeak. She handed the stuffed toy mouse to Lily Mei and Anna Lin. "Here you go! Squeak Squeak's thirsty! He wants some tea!"

The twins ignored her and continued crying. "Maybe we should put on that happy-babies CD," Bess suggested.

Margaret, Lacie, and Matt came into the living room, carrying muffins and glasses of lemonade. "Mom, can we use the family computer to do some research for our science project?" Margaret said.

"Super Sonic Man's gonna put the bad guys in jail!" Cal yelled. The twins cried even more loudly. Sir Barkalot increased his volume too.

"Mom? Like now?" Margaret persisted.

"Margaret, can't you see I'm kind of busy?" Mrs. Jacobs snapped.

"Cal, give the babies their rattle or we're going to have to have a time-out!" Mrs. Jacobs exclaimed.

"*Their* rattle?" Margaret grumbled.

"It's not a *rattle*, it's a *treasure*," Cal corrected everyone.

The chaos and confusion went on for a while, until finally, Mrs. Gregory put on the *Happy Baby Songs* CD, and the twins calmed down and started twirling in place. Cal dropped the silver rattle and started dancing too. Margaret, Lacie, and Matt went upstairs to Margaret's room. Sir Barkalot trotted after them, sniffing at the muffins. Mrs. Jacobs picked up the rattle and put it back on the bookshelf, next to a row of encyclopedias. Then she and Mrs. Gregory sank wearily onto the couch and began talking about an upcoming neighborhood meeting.

Nancy, George, and Bess danced with the twins and Cal until around four thirty, when he and his mother left. "Oh, my gosh! Margaret wanted me to help her log on to the family computer, didn't she?" Mrs. Jacobs said as she closed the front door after them. She rushed upstairs.

Nancy and her friends played with the twins for a little while longer, first making a castle out of the blocks, and then reading books until it was almost time to go home. Just before five, Nancy and George started picking up the toys while Bess finished reading to the twins.

Nancy frowned as she returned Squeak Squeak to the bookshelf. "Where's the silver rattle?" she asked George. "I thought I saw Mrs. Gregory put it here somewhere. Did you move it?"

"Wa-ttle!" Anna Lin repeated

"Wa-ttle!" George smiled at Anna Lin, then turned to Nancy and shook her head. "I didn't move it."

"I didn't move it either," Bess piped up.

Nancy scanned the entire bookshelf. There were books, CDs, a CD player, and toys. But no silver rattle.

Where could it be?

ChaPTER, ThRee

A Green Clue

Did the rattle disappear? Nancy wondered. Or was it just hiding somewhere in the living room, like Lily Mei earlier with her peek-a-boo game?

"I'll look for it," George offered. "Maybe it's under the couch or something."

Nancy nodded. "Okay. I'll go over the bookshelf one more time."

". . . and the beautiful princess said to the sea fairies, 'How many wishes do I have left?'" Bess read to the twins. "No, Anna Lin, Lily Mei gets to turn the page this time," she said firmly.

George searched under the couch, the love seat, and the coffee table. Nancy searched the bookshelf again, more carefully this time. She tried to remember the exact moment when Mrs. Jacob placed the rattle on the shelf. Things had been so crazy, with Cal running around the living room with the rattle . . . Mrs. Gregory telling him to stop . . . the twins crying . . . Mrs. Jacobs trying to comfort them . . . and then Margaret and her friends showing up wanting to use the family computer. Then Mrs. Gregory had played the *Happy Baby Songs* CD, and the twins had started dancing . . . and Cal had dropped the rattle on the floor and joined them.

Nancy closed her eyes, concentrating. In her mind, she saw Mrs. Jacobs plucking the rattle from the floor and putting it . . . where?

Next to the encyclopedias, she remembered suddenly.

Nancy opened her eyes and went over to the long row of encyclopedias, which were on the third shelf from the top. If her memory was right, Mrs. Jacobs had put the rattle near the middle of the row, with the *L*, *M*, and *N* volumes.

Nancy had to stand a little bit on her tippy-toes to reach the encyclopedias. She looked up and down the shelf.

But the rattle wasn't there. Nancy sighed in frustration.

Then she did a double take. On the shelf right in front of the *L*, *M*, and *N* volumes was a smudgy fingerprint. A smudgy *green* fingerprint.

Nancy's thoughts began racing. Could someone have taken the rattle from this spot? And could that someone have had yucky green fingers?

"'You have two wishes left,' the sea fairies said to the princess," Bess was reading to the twins. "Did you guys find *it* yet?" she called out to Nancy and George. Nancy noticed that Bess was trying not to say "rattle" in case it might upset the twins.

"Nope," George replied. "I found a doggie bone, a cat toy, and a baby binkie—I mean, *pacifier.*"

"I didn't find *it*, either. But I did find a clue," Nancy said.

"A clue? What kind of clue?" George asked her.

"A green fingerprint," Nancy explained. "It's time to go home now, so we'll have to look for the r—I mean, *it*—again on Wednesday. And maybe we'll find more clues then, too."

On Wednesday after school, Nancy, George, and Bess found the twins waiting eagerly for them at the door.

"I think they really liked you!" Mrs. Jacobs said, opening the door to let the girls inside. "I told them a few minutes ago that you were coming, and they were so excited."

"That's great!" Bess said. "Hi, Anna Lin! Hi, Lily Mei!" she said, waving.

The twins grinned and waved back. "Kweek Kweek!" Anna Lin said, holding up the stuffed toy mouse for Bess's inspection. Nancy knew it was Anna Lin because she had a small brown birthmark on her neck, and Lily Mei didn't. Nancy had figured this out just before leaving the Jacobses' house on Monday.

"That's right, that's Squeak Squeak," Mrs. Jacobs said.

"Kweek Kweek!" Lily Mei cried out, grabbing for the toy.

"No, no, Lily Mei. Anna Lin is playing with Squeak Squeak now. You have to wait your turn," Mrs. Jacobs told her.

"Kweek Kweek!" Lily Mei yelled angrily.

"Oh, dear. Okay, time for a new activity. Why don't you girls take the twins into the living room and play trains with them for a bit?" Mrs. Jacobs suggested. "I brought their train set down from their room. And, by the way . . . did you put the little silver R-A-T-T-L-E somewhere when you left on Monday?"

"No, we were looking for it too," Nancy replied as they all walked into the living room.

"We think it's missing," George piped up.

"But we can find it for you," Bess added. "Nancy and George and I have a detective club called the Clue Crew, and we're really good at finding stuff."

Mrs. Jacobs smiled. "Wow, you're detectives, too? Yes, that would be wonderful if you could find it. As I mentioned before, it's one of the twins' favorite toys. And of course it has sentimental value for me because it was Margaret's when she was little."

"Mrs. Jacobs, did you have something green on your hands on Monday?" Nancy asked her. "You know, like green paint or green food coloring or anything like that?"

Mrs. Jacobs frowned. "Green paint or green coloring? N-no, I don't think so. Why do you ask?"

Before Nancy could answer, the twins started fighting over Squeak Squeak again. "Okay, let's say bye-bye to Squeak Squeak and play with trains!" Mrs. Jacobs said, taking the toy mouse away and putting it on the bookshelf.

The twins started to complain, until Bess settled down on the floor next to the wooden train tracks and guided one of the trains forward. "Chugga-chugga choo-choo!" she said loudly.

"Choo-choo!" Lily Mei repeated.

"Choo-choo!" Anna Lin joined in.

The twins plopped down on the floor next to Bess and reached for the trains. George sat down with them. Soon the four of them were happily playing.

"I have to finish up a load of laundry in the basement, and then I'll be upstairs doing some cleaning," Mrs. Jacobs said. "Just give me a shout if you need me."

"Okay," Nancy said.

While Bess, George, and the twins were occupied with the trains, Nancy decided to see if the smudgy green fingerprint was still there in front of the *L*, *M*, and *N* volumes. It was.

She touched it lightly with her own finger. It felt dry and slightly bumpy. *Hmm*, she thought. *What could it be?*

Just then, the front door opened and Margaret walked in, followed by Lacie and Matt.

"Mah-Mah!" the twins exclaimed. They jumped to their feet and ran to the baby gate. They grabbed the bars of the gate and shook them hard.

"Yeah, hi," Margaret said, barely looking at them.

"Margaret, you should be nicer to them," Lacie scolded her. "Hi, Anna Lin! Hi, Lily Mei! Are you playing with trains today?" she said, stepping into the living room.

"Choo-choo!" the twins said in unison.

"Who's this?" Matt walked over to the bookshelf and picked up Squeak Squeak. "Whoa, it's a mouse! Let's feed it some cheese!" He pretended to offer it a hunk of cheese. The twins clapped and giggled.

"Can we puh-lease go upstairs and work on our

science project already?" Margaret complained.

"Hey, where's my M-Box?" Lacie said suddenly. "It was in my pocket, like, a second ago."

"What's an M-Box?" George asked her.

"It's a tiny little awesome music player with tiny little awesome headphones," Lacie explained. "I got it for my birthday. If I lose it, my parents are gonna be *so* mad!"

"I haven't seen it," Margaret said.

"What about you, Matt?" Lacie asked him.

Matt had his back to everyone and was studying something on the bookshelf. "I haven't seen it either. But I know someone who has," he called over his shoulder.

Lacie peered at him suspiciously. "What are you talking about? Who?"

"The mouse!" Matt whirled around and held up Squeak Squeak, who had a pair of tiny little headphones attached to his ears.

The twins shrieked with laughter.

"You stole my M-Box! You're *so* lame!" Lacie cried out. She grabbed the headphones and M-Box from Matt.

"Sorry. Still, I think this was my best practical joke this week," Matt bragged. "Or maybe *second* best."

"What was the best one, then? When you put ketchup on Dylan's chocolate pudding during lunch? Or when you slipped a fake spider in Keisha's backpack?" Margaret teased him. "What are you, like, five years old?"

"What can I say? I can't help myself." Matt chuckled.

"Okay, well, no more practical jokes today, okay? It's time to get to work, people!" Margaret headed upstairs, and Matt and Lacie followed.

As soon as they were gone, Nancy turned to George and Bess. "I just got an idea," she said in a low, excited voice. "What if *Matt* stole the silver r—I mean, *it*?"

CHAPTER FOUR

The Strange Science Project

"Matt?" George repeated, frowning.

"Why would he steal *it*?" Bess asked Nancy. "He's in sixth grade, right? Those are for babies."

"Or for Cal, who isn't a baby but who was pretending that it was stolen treasure," George reminded Bess. She sat down on the floor and started making a train station out of blocks with the twins.

"Oh yeah, right." Bess nodded.

"Matt likes to play practical jokes," Nancy said. "He said that stealing Lacie's M-Box was his *second* best practical joke this week. What if stealing *it* was his *best*?"

George and Bess looked thoughtful. "Hmm, good point," George agreed.

Nancy glanced upstairs. "Can you two watch the twins for five minutes? I'm going to go up to Margaret's room to see if I can find out anything."

"But they're *in* there!" Bess cried out.

"I'll just listen at the door. I'll be super quiet," Nancy promised.

"What if Mrs. Jacobs comes back and wants to know where you are?" George asked her.

"Um . . . just tell her I'm in the bathroom or something," Nancy said.

Nancy slipped off her shoes so she wouldn't make any noise, in case the second floor didn't have carpeting. Then she stepped over the baby gate into the hallway. There was another baby gate at the bottom of the stairs. She unhooked it, re-hooked it, then walked very quietly up the stairs.

Once on the second floor—there was another baby gate at the *top* of the stairs—Nancy tried to figure out which room was Margaret's. The first door in the hallway was open. Through the doorway she could see a big bed covered with a gold and white comforter and a nightstand piled high with books and magazines. It looked like a grown-up's room.

The next door Nancy came to was also open. Inside were two white cribs, a bunny mobile hanging from the ceiling, and a painted pink chest spilling over with toys. This was definitely the twins' room.

The third door Nancy came to was closed. Taped to the door was a hand-drawn sign that said "MARGARET'S ROOM," and below it, another hand-drawn sign that said, "DO NOT ENTER!!!!!" This was definitely Margaret's room!

Nancy peered up and down the hallway to make sure she was alone. Then she pressed her ear against the door.

There were voices coming from the other side—Margaret's, Lacie's, and Matt's—and also a loud pop song playing on a CD player or a

radio. Because of the music, it was hard for Nancy to hear their conversation. She could only make out a few words here and there.

They seemed to be discussing their science project. Margaret was saying something about the effects of . . . what? Nancy pressed her ear more tightly against the door. Heat? That's what it sounded like: heat. The effects of heat on . . . Nancy thought she heard Margaret say the word "pain." The effects of heat on pain? She thought about this for a moment. She knew that her father sometimes put a heating pad on his elbow when played too much tennis. Was *that* what they were talking about?

Then Margaret and her friends changed the subject. Margaret said something about "stupid" and "twins." Stupid twins? Was Margaret complaining about the twins again? Matt responded with a statement about . . . boys? No, *toys*. Was he talking about toys? Nancy leaned forward eagerly. Maybe Matt was about to brag about stealing one of the twins' toys as a practical joke.

Then someone started blasting what sounded like a hair dryer, and Nancy couldn't hear anything at all.

"Nancy?"

Nancy whipped around. Mrs. Jacobs was coming down the hall toward her, carrying a laundry basket full of folded clothes.

"What are you doing up here?" Mrs. Jacobs asked her curiously. "That's Margaret's room. Why are you standing outside of Margaret's room?"

"I was, uh, looking for the bathroom," Nancy said. She scrunched up her face, trying to look like she was lost.

"Oh, well, that's the next door down. Why didn't you just use the one downstairs?" Mrs. Jacobs said pleasantly.

"I thought someone was using it. The door was closed. I'll see if they're still in there," Nancy said quickly. "Thanks, Mrs. Jacobs!"

She hurried past Mrs. Jacobs and down the stairs. When she reached the front hall, she stepped over the baby gate into the living room. "Guess what?" she started to say to George and Bess. She wanted to tell them about the conversation—or the sort-of-conversation—she'd overheard through Margaret's door.

But Nancy stopped. Something was wrong. George and Bess looked upset, and the twins were whimpering, their cheeks streaked with fresh tears.

"What happened?" Nancy said.

"They wanted Squeak Squeak to ride on the train—" George began.

"But when I went to get him, he was gone!" Bess finished. "Squeak Squeak is missing!"

ChaPTER FiVE

A Furry Suspect

"Squeak Squeak is missing?" Nancy said, surprised. "Since when?"

"Kweek-Kweek!" Anna Lin said, sniffling.

"Since just now," George explained. "He was on the bookshelf before."

Nancy glanced over at the bookshelf. She recalled Mrs. Jacobs taking Squeak Squeak from the twins and placing it there, out of their reach. She also recalled Matt pretending to feed Squeak Squeak cheese, then stealing Lacie's M-Box and fitting the tiny little headphones over the mouse's ears—as a "prank."

"Matt was playing with Squeak Squeak," Nancy reminded her friends.

"Oh yeah, that's right." George nodded.

"Did Matt put Squeak Squeak back on the bookshelf?" Nancy asked.

George frowned. "I don't think so," she said after a moment.

"I *thought* he did," Bess said. "But I'm not totally sure."

"I'm not totally sure either," Nancy admitted.

The twins started crying again. "I'll put on their happy-babies CD," George said, hurrying over to the CD player.

"Good idea. And we can dance with Togo!" Bess said brightly. "Anna Lin, Lily Mei, do you want to meet Togo?"

The twins stopped crying and stared wide-eyed at Bess.

Bess went over to her backpack, which she had left in the hallway. She returned a moment later with the scruffy-looking stuffed tiger.

"Hi, Anna Lin! Hi, Lily Mei! I'm Togo!" Bess said in a deep voice.

"Go-go!" the twins squealed happily.

The CD came on. The twins began twirling, and Bess twirled along with them, holding Togo in the air. *Bess saves the day!* Nancy thought, relieved.

While Bess and Togo danced with the twins, Nancy and George searched the living room for Squeak Squeak. They searched every inch of the bookshelf. They searched under all the furniture. They searched under toys and books and pillows and blankies. But there was no sign of him.

They finally gave up. "*What* is going on?" George said to Nancy in a whisper so the twins wouldn't overhear. "First, someone steals the rattle. Then Squeak Squeak."

"It's definitely a mystery," Nancy agreed.

"Any luck?" Bess called over to them. The

twins were hanging on to the hem of her untucked T-shirt and bouncing up and down to a song called "Let's Tickle Pickles!"

"No. We'll find him, though," Nancy replied.

"So what happened upstairs?" George whispered.

Nancy told George about the conversation she'd overheard through Margaret's bedroom door. "It was kind of hard to figure out what they were talking about," she finished. "But Matt was definitely saying something about 'toys.'"

"Toys as in the silver rattle?" George mused.

"And maybe as in Squeak Squeak, too," Nancy added.

"Do you think the same person took both of them?" George said.

Nancy considered this. "Maybe. Probably. We won't know until we find more clues." She added, "So far, the only clue we have is the green fingerprint."

Just then, Nancy was distracted by a strange

noise. She glanced around the room, wondering what it might be.

It only took a moment for her to find the source of the noise. A big—no, *huge*—orange cat was crouched next to a small blue rug and batting her paws at something.

Nancy pointed to the cat. "That must be Pumpkin Pie."

The twins noticed Pumpkin Pie too. "Meow!" Lily Mae said excitedly.

"Meow, meow!" Anna Lin joined in.

Nancy wondered what Pumpkin Pie was playing with. She seemed to be pawing at a lumpy, bumpy object hidden under the rug.

Curious, Nancy went over and lifted the rug. George followed along. Underneath was a small cat toy, shaped like a bird.

"Is *this* what you're looking for?" Nancy teased the cat. Pumpkin Pie meowed loudly at Nancy and pawed at the toy.

"Pumpkin Pie reminds me of my next-door neighbor's cat, Furball," Nancy told George.

"Furball likes to hide toys under rugs and then find them again."

"Nancy, you're a genius!" George said suddenly.

Nancy smiled. "I am?"

"What if Pumpkin Pie took Squeak Squeak and hid him under a rug somewhere?" George suggested. "And what if she did the same thing with the rattle? Maybe *she's* our thief!"

ChaPTER Six

Hide and Go Seek

"You think Pumpkin Pie might be our thief?" Nancy said to George.

"Maybe. What if she found the rattle and hid it under a rug somewhere? And what if she did the same thing with Squeak Squeak?" George said eagerly.

Bess and the twins were on the other side of the living room, holding hands and dancing in slow circles to a song called "Wave Bye-Bye." "What are you guys talking about?" she called out. "Did you solve the mystery, or what?"

"No, but we have a new suspect," Nancy replied.

"Who?" Bess asked her.

George pointed to the cat. "Pumpkin Pie!"

"Meow!" Anna Lin and Lily Mei said in unison.

"Our thief is a kitty?" Bess said, giggling.

"*Might* be," Nancy corrected her. "I think we should follow her around the house and see if she'll show us more of her hiding places. Maybe we'll find the, um, two missing items."

"That's an awesome plan," George agreed. "Bess, do you want to go with Nancy? I can dance with the twins for a while."

"Sure!" Bess said.

When the next song came on, George took Togo from Bess and started dancing with the twins while Nancy and Bess trailed after Pumpkin Pie. First, the big orange cat led them to the kitchen, where she scarfed down a bowl of tuna-flavored kibbles. Then she led them to the dining room, on the other side of the kitchen. There, she began batting her paw at a lumpy, bumpy object under a small gold rug.

"Hey, maybe that's the rattle!" Nancy said excitedly.

"Or maybe that's Squeak Squeak!" Bess added.

Nancy and Bess got down on their hands and knees and lifted up the small gold rug. They both sneezed as cat fur and dust tickled their noses.

"Can you—*achoo!*—reach it?" Bess said.

"I think so." Nancy extended her hand and touched the object. It felt cold and hard, like metal. "Yay, it's the rattle!" she announced, pulling it out. "No, it's not the rattle. Sorry! It's just a soup spoon."

Pumpkin Pie pawed at the spoon. "Okay, Pumpkin Pie. Take us to your other super-secret hiding places," Nancy told her.

It took a while, but eventually Pumpkin Pie trotted through a doorway and down a set of stairs. "She's going down to the basement," Bess said as she and Nancy followed behind. "Basements are dark and scary. They're really good hiding places!"

"Well, this basement's not so dark and scary," Nancy noted when they reached the bottom of the stairs. Before them was a large family room with bright yellow walls, dark brown furniture, a pool table, and a large plasma-screen TV. There were toys scattered across the thick beige carpeting. "But maybe Pumpkin Pie hid the rattle and Squeak Squeak down here, anyway."

"Maybe!" Bess agreed.

But after a few minutes of following Pumpkin Pie and checking out all the lumpy, bumpy objects she pawed at, Nancy and Bess turned up empty-handed. The only items they found were a couple of catnip balls, a hair scrunchie, a pack of gum, and an empty sippy cup.

"Now what?" Bess asked Nancy. "We followed

Pumpkin Pie all over the first floor and the basement. Should we follow her all over the second floor, too?"

Nancy glanced at her watch. "We can't. It's almost time to go. We'll have to wait until Friday." She smiled and added: "Besides, Hannah is taking us all out for pizza tonight!"

"Let's get a pizza with extra pepperoni!" Nancy suggested.

"Let's get a pizza with extra everything!" Bess piped up.

"Extra everything sounds good to me!" George agreed.

"You girls must be pretty hungry," Hannah Gruen remarked, shutting her menu.

"We are! We've been working on a really, *really* hard case," Bess told her.

Hannah grinned. "A really, *really* hard case? I want to hear all about it."

The four of them were sitting in a booth at Pizza Paradise, in downtown River Heights.

Nancy loved it when Hannah brought them there. In Nancy's humble opinion, Pizza Paradise had the yummiest pizza in the whole world.

Hannah was the Drews' housekeeper. But she did a lot more than take care of the Drews' house. She had been taking care of Nancy since her mother died five years ago. She gave great hugs, she brushed Nancy's hair every day, and she was the queen of homemade lasagna. Nancy thought of her as one of the family.

The waitress brought a pitcher of ginger ale and four glasses, then took their pizza order. As soon as she was gone, Nancy and the girls filled Hannah in on the case.

"So someone stole a silver baby rattle and a toy mouse, huh?" Hannah said when they had finished. "That's pretty mean!"

"Someone or some*thing*," George corrected her. "One of our suspects is Pumpkin Pie."

Hannah frowned, confused. "One of your suspects is a pie?"

Nancy giggled. "No, Hannah! Pumpkin Pie is a cat! She likes to hide stuff under rugs."

"That's a funny name for a cat," Hannah said, chuckling. "So who are your other suspects, besides this Pumpkin Pie?"

"Well, there's Margaret's friend Matt," Bess said, taking a sip of her soda. "He likes to play practical jokes."

"*And* he was at the Jacobses' house on Monday when the rattle disappeared, and on Wednesday when Squeak Squeak disappeared," George added.

Nancy listened as Bess and George told Hannah about Matt. As she listened, something occurred to her. There was another suspect they should have added to the list. Why hadn't they considered him before? "What about Cal?" Nancy said out loud.

Bess and George both turned to her. "What *about* Cal?" Bess asked.

"He was there on Monday when the rattle disappeared. He took it from the twins, remember?"

Nancy pointed out. "The only problem is . . . he wasn't there on Wednesday when Squeak Squeak disappeared."

"Maybe there are *two* thieves," George pointed out.

"Or maybe Cal flew in and out of the Jacobses' house on Wednesday using his Super Sonic Man powers and nobody saw him," Bess joked. Everyone laughed.

"So do you have any clues yet?" Hannah asked.

"We found a green fingerprint where the rattle was supposed to be," Nancy replied. "It's our only clue we have so far. But we'll find more!"

"I know you will," Hannah said, smiling. "After all, you're the Clue Crew!"

"Are we late?" Bess asked Nancy and George as they half walked, half ran down the sidewalk toward the Jacobses' house.

"No, but we're almost late. We'd better hurry," Nancy replied.

The three girls increased their speed as the Jacobses' red-shuttered house came into view. It was Friday, and they were running behind because there had been a fire drill at school, which had delayed the afternoon dismissal.

"Yay, we're not late. We're one minute early!" Nancy announced when they got to the Jacobses' door and rang the bell.

A moment later, Mrs. Jacobs opened the door.

Behind her, Nancy could hear the twins crying. Mrs. Jacobs looked exhausted—and worried.

"Are Anna Lin and Lily Mei okay?" Nancy asked immediately.

"Oh, they're upset because Squeak Squeak is still missing," Mrs. Jacobs replied, watching the twins over her shoulder. Nancy had told her about the disappearance of the toy mouse before she, George, and Bess went home on Wednesday. "I thought I would cheer them up by playing their *Happy Baby Songs* CD. But—" She hesitated.

"But what?" George prompted her.

"But now, the CD is missing too!" Mrs. Jacobs told them.

ChAPTER SEVEN

Another Clue

Nancy gasped. "The CD is missing too?"

"Since when?" Bess piped up.

"I'm not sure," Mrs. Jacobs said.

"When was the last time you saw it?" Nancy asked her.

Mrs. Jacobs thought for a moment. "Yesterday, I think, around five," she said finally.

She waved the girls inside and closed the door. The four of them joined the twins in the living room.

Bess reached into her backpack and whipped out Togo the tiger. "Hi, Anna Lin! Hi, Lily Mei! Do you want to play with blocks?" she asked in her deep Togo voice.

The twins snuffled and regarded Togo. After a moment, Anna Lin reached for Togo and gave him a big, sloppy kiss. Lily Mei gave him a kiss too, then plopped down on the floor and began stacking blocks.

Mrs. Jacobs smiled affectionately at her daughters. "So as I was saying," she said in a low voice to Nancy, George, and Bess, "the last time I saw the CD was around five yesterday. I'd been playing it for the twins. I was just about to put it back in its case when the doorbell rang. It was Sarah—Mrs. Gregory—and her son, Cal. I remember putting the CD on top of the CD player so I could get the door. I kind of forgot about it after that."

Nancy frowned. Now there were three things missing: the silver rattle, Squeak Squeak, and the *Happy Baby Songs* CD. What was going on? Was this the work of one thief? Or two? Or maybe even three?

Nancy walked over to the CD player, which was on the bookshelf one shelf down from the encyclopedias. She recognized the case lying on top of the CD player, with its picture of several smiling babies against a tropical rain forest background, and the title *Happy Baby Songs* in bright orange and purple letters.

Nancy picked up the case and opened it. It was empty—just like Mrs. Jacobs said. She remembered then that her father sometimes put CDs back in the wrong cases. Just to be 100 percent sure, she did a quick sweep of all the CD cases on the bookshelf. There were thirty of them, total. But none of them contained the *Happy Baby Songs* CD. She also hit the Eject button on the CD player, in case the CD was still in there. It wasn't.

And then Nancy saw something she hadn't noticed before. On top of the CD player, where she had found the *Happy Baby Songs* case, was a smudgy fingerprint.

But this time, it wasn't green. It was yellow.

Nancy turned around. George and Bess were still playing blocks with the twins. Mrs. Jacobs was straightening a pile of magazines on the coffee table.

"Mrs. Jacobs? Did you have something yellow on your fingers yesterday? Or anytime this week?" Nancy asked her.

Mrs. Jacobs frowned. "Something *yellow* on my fingers? No, not that I can think of. Let's see . . . yesterday, I made some cupcakes for a bake sale at Margaret's school. But I used white frosting, not yellow."

Nancy thought about this. "Were, um, Matt and Lacie here yesterday after school?" she asked after a moment.

Mrs. Jacobs nodded. "Yes, to work on their science project. They've been here every day this week."

Just then, the phone rang. "Excuse me," Mrs. Jacobs said, heading toward the kitchen.

Nancy studied the yellow fingerprint for a few more minutes. She touched it lightly. It felt similar to the smudgy green fingerprint, dry and slightly bumpy.

She stood on her tippy-toes and peered at the shelf with the row of encyclopedias, at the spot in front of the *L*, *M*, and *N* volumes. The smudgy green fingerprint was still there.

I guess the thief didn't come back to get rid of the evidence, Nancy thought. *Or maybe he—or she—didn't know it was there.*

Nancy heard Sir Barkalot barking. She turned around just in time to see him leaping over the baby gate and into the living room. He stopped in his tracks as his eyes zeroed in on Togo, who was perched in the floor between the twins. He looked as though he was hungry for a snack.

A stuffed toy tiger snack! Nancy thought, alarmed.

"Bess! George! Hide Togo before the dog eats him!" Nancy shouted.

Bess grabbed Togo quickly and stuffed under her T-shirt. "You stay away from Togo, you bad dog!" she chided Sir Barkalot, who ran up to her and started sniffing at her T-shirt. "You're supposed to be eating doggie food, not . . ."

Bess didn't finish her sentence. She turned to George and Nancy with a triumphant grin. "I think I just solved our mystery!" she announced.

CHAPTER EIGHT

A Clue Crew Sleepover

"What do you mean you solved the mystery?" Nancy asked Bess.

"You figured out who the thief is?" George piped up. "Tell us!"

Bess grinned. She reached out and patted Sir Barkalot, who was still sniffing at her T-shirt in search of Togo. "It's Sir Barkalot!" she exclaimed. "*He's* our thief!"

"Sir Barkalot?" Nancy and George said in unison.

Bess nodded. "Uh-huh. Remember what Mrs. Jacobs told us on Monday? That Sir Barkalot eats everything, including CDs?"

"Oh, yeah . . . ," George said slowly. "So you think—"

"Sir Barkalot ate the *Happy Baby Songs* CD," Bess finished. "He may have eaten the you-know-what and the other you-know-what, too," she added, lowering her voice and casting a worried glance at the twins. But the babies were too busy petting Sir Barkalot to pay attention to what Bess and her friends were talking about.

Nancy considered Bess's idea. "Mrs. Jacobs said Sir Barkalot *tries* to eat everything. She didn't say he actually *ate* CDs," she reminded Bess.

"Hmm, good point," Bess admitted. "There's one way to find out for sure, though." She leaned forward and blew a puff of air at Sir Barkalot's snout.

George frowned, looking totally confused. "Why are you blowing on Sir Barkalot?" she asked Bess. Nancy was confused too.

Sir Barkalot let out a great big yawn. Bess leaned forward and peeked quickly into his open mouth. "I'm making him yawn! I wanted to see if there are tiny little CD pieces stuck in his teeth!"

"Oh!" Nancy said. She had never heard of

trying to make a
dog yawn this
way. "Um . . .
so are there?"

Bess
squinted,
trying to see. She shook her

head just as Sir Barkalot clamped his mouth shut. "No," she said, sounding disappointed. "But there's another way to find out if he ate the CD."

"What?" George asked her.

Bess inched closer to Sir Barkalot and started massaging his stomach. "I'm going to see if I can feel the CD in there," she said, kneading her hands into his tummy.

"Ew," Nancy groaned.

"Double ew," George agreed.

But Sir Barkalot didn't want to cooperate with the doggie massage. He yipped loudly at Bess, then took off running toward the kitchen.

"Hey, our thief is getting away!" George joked. "Catch him!"

Bess made a face at her. "Ha-ha. *I* still think we should add him to the suspect list. After all, *you* added Pumpkin Pie, right?"

"Yeah, that's true," George conceded. "Okay, so we'll add Sir Barkalot. I guess there's no reason we can't have *two* pets as suspects!"

"Pass the popcorn!" Bess said. She plopped down cross-legged on top of Nancy's bed. Her lavender pajamas were the same color as the bedspread.

"Hannah put nacho cheese flavoring on it," Nancy said, passing the bowl to Bess. "It's super yummy!" Her pajamas were white with turquoise and yellow polka dots.

"Save some for me!" George said. She was sitting in front of Nancy's computer, typing. Instead of regular pajamas, she wore a green soccer jersey over gray leggings. "I'm starting a new file with our suspect list and clues."

It was Friday night, and the three girls were having a sleepover at Nancy's house. They'd already had a big do-it-yourself taco dinner with Hannah and Nancy's dad, Carson Drew. After two big tacos apiece, Nancy was surprised that she, George, and Bess still had room for popcorn, hot apple cider, and Hannah's homemade brownies. But they did!

Nancy's dog, Chocolate Chip, was curled up on the shaggy lavender rug, napping. Every once in a while she opened her eyes and sniffed at the air to see if there might be any popcorn kernels or brownie crumbs that had fallen to the floor.

Nancy set her mug of apple cider on her nightstand, then got up and stood next to George to see what she was typing. George was typing from some notes about the case that Nancy had written down in a special blue notebook:

THE CASE OF THE MISSING BABY STUFF
— WHAT'S MISSING —

❀ A silver rattle shaped like a moon. It's one of the twins' favorite toys. It disappeared on Monday after school.

❀ A toy mouse named Squeak Squeak. It's

one of the twins' favorite toys too. It disappeared on Wednesday after school.

❀ The twins' favorite CD, called *Happy Baby Songs*. It probably disappeared sometime between Thursday at 5 p.m. (when Mrs. Gregory and Cal came over) and Friday before 3 p.m. (when we got to the house).

— SUSPECTS —

❀ Matt: Margaret's friend. Matt and their other friend Lacie come over every day after school to work on a science project with Margaret. Matt likes to play practical jokes. He was at the house on Monday when the rattle disappeared. He was also at the house on Wednesday when Squeak Squeak disappeared. Nancy heard him talking about toys right around the time Squeak Squeak disappeared. He was also at the house on Thursday when the CD (probably) disappeared.

✤ Cal: The neighbor's little boy. He thinks he's Super Sonic Man (ha-ha). He took the twins' rattle on Monday when he and his mom came over to the house. He could have stolen the rattle (again) before he and his mom left. He was there at the house on Thursday when the CD (probably) disappeared. But he wasn't at the house on Wednesday when Squeak Squeak disappeared.

✤ Pumpkin Pie: A cat! She likes to take stuff and bury it under rugs.

✤ Sir Barkalot: A dog! He likes to try to eat stuff like toys and CDs.

— CLUES —

✤ We found a <u>green</u> fingerprint near where the rattle disappeared.

✤ We found a <u>yellow</u> fingerprint near where the CD disappeared.

Nancy read George's typed notes two whole times. "This is great," she said when she was finished. She pointed to the part about Pumpkin Pie. "Bess and I were going to follow her around the house some more today. But Mrs. Jacobs said she was at the Purrfect Pets Salon, getting groomed. We'll have to wait until Monday."

George pointed to the part about Sir Barkalot. "On Monday, we should ask Mrs. Jacobs if he was sick this weekend—or anytime last week. I mean, if he swallowed the CD or the rattle or Squeak Squeak, he'd have a really bad tummy ache, right?"

"Good point," Bess agreed, munching on a handful of popcorn.

Nancy pointed to the part about the clues. "I wish we could figure out what these clues mean. Why did the thief have green fingers on Monday? And then yellow fingers on Thursday or Friday?"

"*Hey!*" Bess jumped up from the bed, almost spilling the entire bowl of nacho cheese-flavored popcorn. A few kernels dropped to the floor and were hastily scarfed down by Chocolate Chip. "I just remembered something else Mrs. Jacobs told

us on Monday," Bess
went on. "You know, when
she was telling us about the
twins and stuff?

She said that the
twins liked to finger paint, right?"

"Yup," Nancy said.

"Hmm. Are you saying that the green and
yellow fingerprints might be from finger paint?"
George asked her cousin.

Bess's blue eyes sparkled with excitement.
"Yes! And what if the green and yellow fingerprints are from Anna Lin and Lily Mei? What if
they're the thieves?"

Chapter Nine

Three Down

"Anna Lin and Lily Mei?" Nancy said, surprised. "You think *they're* the thieves?"

"But why would they steal their own toys and stuff?" George asked Bess.

Bess shrugged. "Maybe they didn't *steal* them. Maybe they just took them when no one was looking and put them somewhere, and they can't remember where. But they don't know how to tell their mom because they don't know a lot of words."

Nancy sat down on the bed and thought about this. "There's only one problem with your theory," she told Bess after a moment. "The twins are too short!"

"Huh?" Bess said, puzzled.

"The rattle was on the bookshelf when it disappeared, right next to the encyclopedias," Nancy pointed out. "I have to stand on my tippy-toes to reach that shelf, and I'm way taller than the twins. The CD was on top of the CD player when it disappeared. That's one shelf below, but that's still pretty high." She added, "We're not exactly sure where Squeak Squeak was when he disappeared. Maybe the bookshelf—maybe not."

George's eyes lit up. "That means there's no way Cal could have reached those shelves either."

"Or Pumpkin Pie . . . or Sir Barkalot," Bess said. "Unless Pumpkin Pie can jump that high."

"I just thought of something else that doesn't make sense with Pumpkin Pie and Sir Barkalot," Nancy said suddenly. "They couldn't have left the green fingerprint or the yellow fingerprint."

George and Bess both stared at her. "Oh, yeah. Why didn't we think of that before?" George exclaimed.

"This case would be a lot easier to solve if

the thief had left green and yellow *paw* prints instead," Bess joked.

George swiveled around in the chair and frowned at the computer screen. "Hey, guys? Guess what. We've just crossed out most of the suspects on our suspect list," she noted.

"Except for Matt," Nancy said.

"He's definitely got to be our thief," Bess agreed. "Let's go arrest him right this second! Well, not arrest him, but you know what I mean."

"Let's wait until Monday after school," Nancy suggested. "He'll probably be at their house working on the science project, right? We can ask him some questions."

"A *lot* of questions," George said, narrowing her eyes. "If he's our thief, we have to make sure he 'fesses up. Stealing stuff from babies is a really mean thing to do. We can't let him get away with it!"

"Hi, girls! Come in!"

Mrs. Jacobs greeted Nancy, George, and Bess

at the door on Monday after school. She was holding Anna Lin in one arm and Lily Mei in the other. The twins started flapping their hands excitedly when they saw Nancy and her friends.

"Hi, Mrs. Jacobs. Hi, Anna Lin! Hi, Lily Mei!" Nancy said.

"Go-go!" Anna Lin cried out, reaching for Bess.

"Don't worry, I brought Togo. He's taking a cozy little nap in here," Bess said, patting her backpack.

The girls followed Mrs. Jacobs into the living room. Once there, she set the twins down on the floor. They sat down and began digging through a basket of books. George and Bess sat down with them. "How about *The Very Funny Bunny*?" Bess suggested. "Togo can read it with us!"

Nancy turned to Mrs. Jacobs. "Are the . . . three things still missing?" she asked in a low voice. She didn't want to say the words "rattle," "Squeak Squeak," or "*Happy Baby Songs*" out loud, in case the twins might overhear.

Mrs. Jacobs nodded, her expression troubled.

"I'm afraid so. Have you had any luck, you know, with your detective work?"

"We've got some ideas," Nancy replied. Then she remembered to ask Mrs. Jacobs George's question about Sir Barkalot. He wasn't high on their suspect list anymore, but it was worth asking, anyway. "Mrs. Jacobs? Did Sir Barkalot have a tummy ache this weekend? Or maybe last week?"

"A tummy ache? N-no," Mrs. Jacobs replied.

"That's good," Nancy said. "I guess he didn't eat the CD or other two missing things, then."

Mrs. Jacobs laughed. "No, I guess not. But considering what a big eater he is, that's a very good theory!"

Nancy heard the sound of a door closing upstairs. "Are Matt and Lacie here?" she asked Mrs. Jacobs.

"Yes, they are. They're all working hard on their science project," Mrs. Jacobs said. "Excuse me, I have to check on my lasagna." She bent down and kissed the twins on the tops of their heads, then headed toward the kitchen.

Anna Lin was curled up on George's lap, and Lily Mei was curled up on Bess's. Togo was sitting between them, in front of their book. "Can you keep reading to them? I'm going to go talk to Matt," Nancy said to her friends.

"And Brother Bunny said to Sister Bunny, 'Give me back my super-special magic carrot!'" Bess read. She glanced up at Nancy. "Are you sure you'll be okay all by yourself? What if Matt tries to escape? What if he's a dangerous criminal? What if—"

"I'll be okay," Nancy cut in, giggling.

Nancy headed upstairs and proceeded to Margaret's room. The door was closed, with the same signs as before—"MARGARET'S ROOM" and "DO NOT ENTER!!!!!"—as well as a new one that said, "THAT MEANS YOU, ANNA LIN AND LILY MEI!!!!!"

Nancy pressed her ear against the door and heard the familiar voices of Margaret, Lacie, and Matt. She smiled to herself. Unlike last

Wednesday, there was no music playing from a CD player or radio. She could hear every word they were saying.

"So things are going really well, right?" Margaret was saying.

"Oh, yeah! Three down, three to go," Matt replied.

Nancy frowned. *Three down, three to go?*

By "three down," was Matt referring to the silver rattle, Squeak Squeak, and the CD?

By "three to go," did he mean he planned on stealing three *more* things from the twins?

ChaPTER TEN

Happy Babies

Nancy's mind was racing. What was Matt up to? Did he really intend to steal again . . . and again . . . and again . . . from the twins? She knew he loved playing practical jokes. But why couldn't he leave the poor little babies alone and pick on someone his own age?

And then another thing occurred to her. He had said "three down, three to go" to Margaret and Lacie. Did that mean they were in on this too? Or was he just bragging to them?

Nancy realized just then that Margaret, Lacie, and Matt had stopped talking. There was a long silence. She scrunched up more tightly against the door, wondering if they had lowered their voices.

Just then, the door opened. Nancy practically fell into Margaret's room.

"Aha! I *knew* I heard a noise!" Margaret shouted. "You were spying on us. Why? Did Dylan send you here?"

Nancy scrambled to her feet and smoothed

her hair. She could feel a blush creeping into her cheeks. It wasn't going to be easy explaining this. "Um, Dylan who?" she asked, trying to sound casual.

"Dylan Shaw. He's been trying to find out the results of our top-secret science project," Lacie spoke up. "Are you and your friends working for him or what?"

"N-no," Nancy stammered.

"Then what were you doing?" Margaret demanded.

Nancy took a second to collect her thoughts. Standing in the open doorway, she glanced around Margaret's room, which was blue and white and had posters of horses on the walls. The floor was cluttered with paint-splattered canvases, a hair dryer, an iron and ironing board, and various jars, pots, plates, and brushes. Nancy guessed that this was the equipment for their science project.

Her gaze settled on Margaret, Lacie, and Matt, who were standing together in the middle of the room. They were waiting for her explanation.

Nancy gulped. "Your sisters are missing some stuff," she said, addressing her comments to Margaret. "The silver rattle, Squeak Squeak, and their happy-babies CD. Your mom asked George and Bess and me to try to find them."

Margaret's eyes grew big. "She did?"

"Yup. I came upstairs because I have some questions for Matt," Nancy went on.

Matt looked surprised. "Me? What did I do?"

Nancy turned to him. "Did *you* steal the toys and the CD from Anna Lin and Lily Mei?" she demanded.

Matt cracked up. "Uh, no way. That's crazy! Why would I do that?"

"Because you like playing practical jokes," Nancy said. "Besides, you were here when all three things disappeared. Plus, what did you mean just now when you said, 'three down, three to go'?"

"Huh? Oh, *that*. I was talking about our science project," Matt replied.

"Yeah. We're studying the effect of heat on paint," Lacie piped up.

Heat on paint, *not* pain, Nancy thought.

"We're studying how heat affects different colors of house paint," Matt went on. "You know, like does blue dry faster than orange? Does white crack and peel at the same temperature as red? Each of us is in charge of two different colors."

"I'm in charge of red and orange," Lacie said. "Matt's in charge of blue and white. Margaret's in charge of green and yellow. So far, we've done green, yellow, and red. That's three down. We have three colors to go."

Nancy took a deep breath. "You're in charge of the green and yellow paint?" she said to Margaret.

Margaret folded her arms across her chest. "Yeah. So?"

Nancy thought about the green fingerprint on the bookshelf and the yellow fingerprint on the CD player. Margaret had been in the house every day last week. Margaret had had the same opportunities to steal the twins' things as Matt—and more.

Nancy heard footsteps behind her. She turned to see George and Bess. George was carrying Anna Lin in her arms. Bess was carrying Lily Mei.

"They were asking for you," George told Margaret.

"So we thought we'd come up and visit," Bess added.

"Your timing's perfect," Nancy said. She turned and regarded Margaret. "*You* took the twins' things," she said slowly. Behind her, she heard both George and Bess gasp.

Margaret's jaw dropped. "I did not!" she said angrily.

"I think you did," Nancy persisted. "You left evidence. There was a green fingerprint on the bookshelf where the silver rattle was. And there was a yellow fingerprint on the CD player where the *Happy Baby Songs* CD was."

"You're lying! You're making it up, and . . ." Margaret stopped. She glanced at the twins, then dropped her eyes to the ground. "Um. Okay, well, maybe I did kind of take that stuff," she whispered.

"Margaret, that's so mean!" Lacie scolded her.

"Yeah, dude, that's even meaner than something *I* would do," Matt added.

"Well, they deserved it," Margaret said miserably. "Everything was fine until they came to live with us! Mom and Dad are so stressed lately, taking care of them. And they take *my* stuff, too! That silver rattle is mine!"

Anna Lin wriggled out of George's arms. Lily Mei did the same with Bess. The two babies ran toward Margaret and hugged her. "Mah-git!" Anna Lin exclaimed happily.

"Mah-git!" Lily Mei joined in. She planted a big, sticky kiss on Margaret's leg.

Margaret's expression softened into a smile. "Oh! Hey! You guys said my name!"

"Mah-git!" the twins repeated.

"Margaret, give them back their stuff right now," Matt ordered her.

"Yeah, okay." Margaret took the twins by the hands and led them to her dresser. She opened the top drawer and pulled out the silver rattle, Squeak Squeak, and the CD. "Here you go. Sorry, okay?" she apologized to her sisters. "I guess I've gotta say I'm sorry to my parents, too."

Anna Lin began jumping up and down. "Kweek Kweek!"

Lily Mei grabbed the silver rattle and shook it back and forth. "Wa-ttle!"

Nancy turned and grinned at George and Bess. "Well, we don't have to follow Pumpkin Pie around the house anymore," she joked.

"And I don't have to give Sir Barkalot

any more tummy massages," Bess added.

The three girls laughed.

That night, before going to sleep Nancy curled up in bed and wrote in her special purple notebook:

Today, the Clue Crew solved "The Case of the Missing Baby Stuff." It turned out that Margaret was jealous of her baby sisters. So she took the silver rattle and Squeak Squeak and the happy-babies CD.

She said "I'm sorry" to them and to her mom, too. Her mom was mad at first. But then she said she should spend more time with Margaret and pay more attention to her.

When we left their house, Margaret was playing tea party with the twins. It was her idea and everything. Maybe she'll start being nicer to them from now on?

I don't know which is more fun, being a detective or being a babysitter!

You Can Become a Mother's Helper Too!

Nancy, George, and Bess had so much fun helping Mrs. Jacobs take care of Anna Lin and Lily Mei.

If you're responsible, creative, patient, and like playing with younger children, maybe you could be a good mother's helper too! Always be sure to ask your parents' permission before you start.

A personalized mother's helper notebook will help you keep track of your appointments as well as the families you will be helping.

You Will Need:

A small spiral-bound or hardcover
  notebook
Pens and Magic Markers
Stickers

❀ With a pen or Magic Marker, write MY MOTHER'S HELPER NOTEBOOK (or any title you choose) on the cover of the notebook.

❀ Decorate the outside (and inside) of the notebook with cute stickers and drawings.

❀ Inside, save a separate page (or several pages) for each mother's helper job you have. Use the pages to keep track of the following:

- Name and age of the child (or children)

- Name of parent or parents

- Address and phone number (including parents' cell phone numbers)

- The days and hours you'll be working as a mother's helper for the family

- Your mother's helper duties

- Special things you need to know about the child

- *Important:* If one of your jobs will be to feed the child snacks, make sure you know what snacks are okay and what snacks are not.

❀ Don't forget to bring your special notebook to all your mother's helper jobs and take down notes whenever you learn something new!

Mermaid Tales

Exciting under-the-sea adventures with
Shelly and her mermaid friends!

MermaidTalesBooks.com

Candy Fairies

Chocolate Dreams

Rainbow Swirl

Caramel Moon

Cool Mint

Magic Hearts

Gooey Goblins

The Sugar Ball

A Valentine's Surprise

Visit
candyfairies.com
for more delicious
fun with your
favorite fairies.

31901064780473

Play games, download activities, and so much more!